JAMBERRY

JAMBERRY

story and pictures by
Bruce Degen

HarperCollins*Publishers*

Jamberry

Copyright - 1983 , 2000 by Bruce Degen

This 2008 edition licensed for publication by Barnes & Noble Publishing, Inc., by
HarperCollins Publishers.

HarperCollins Publishers - is a registered trademark.

Barnes & Noble Publishing, Inc.
122 Fifth Avenue
New York, NY 10011

ISBN 13: 978-1-4351-0992-6
ISBN 10: 1-4351-0992-9
Manufactured in China.
08 09 10 11 MCH 10 9 8 7 6 5 4 3 2 1

For my special Berry Picker
and the two Little Berries

ne berry
Two berry
Pick me a blueberry

Hatberry
Shoeberry
In my canoeberry

Under the bridge
And over the dam
Looking for berries
Berries for jam

Three berry
Four berry
Hayberry
Strawberry

Finger and pawberry
My berry, your berry

Strawberry ponies
Strawberry lambs
Dancing in meadows
Of strawberry jam

Quickberry!
Quackberry!
Pick me a blackberry!

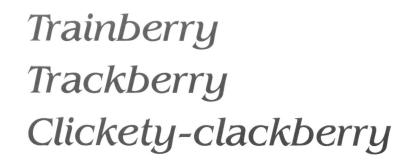

Trainberry
Trackberry
Clickety-clackberry

Rumble and ramble
In blackberry bramble
Billions of berries
For blackberry jamble

Raspberry
Jazzberry
Razzamatazzberry
Berryband
Merryband
Jamming in Berryland

Raspberry rabbits
Brassberry band
Elephants skating
On raspberry jam

Moonberry
Starberry
Cloudberry sky

Boomberry
Zoomberry
Rockets shoot by

Mountains and fountains
Rain down on me
Buried in berries
What a jam jamboree!

When I was a little boy, berries never came from a store. We found them in the fields. Grandma would take a pot, Grandpa would take a can, and I would take my pail. We picked and picked and didn't come home until we had filled them up with berries. Then we would sit in the kitchen and eat fresh washed berries with sour cream and sugar, while the house filled with the warm smell of blueberry pie in the oven and blackberry jam cooking on the stove.

I still love looking for berries in fields. But now my wife and two sons and I do the picking. We fill cans and pots and pails with berries and then have a feast of pies and jams and berries with lots of cream!

Bruce Degen